This is me – Nicholas.

This is my dad.

This is our new pet (having a bath).

And here come the police – oh dear, trouble!

Jeremy Strong once worked in a bakery, putting the jam into three thousand doughnuts every night. Now he puts the jam in stories instead, which he finds much more exciting. At the age of three, he fell out of a first-floor bedroom window and landed on his head. His mother says that this damaged him for the rest of his life and refuses to take any responsibility. He loves writing stories because he says it is 'the only time you alone have complete control and can make anything happen'. His ambition is to make you laugh (or at least snuffle). Jeremy Strong lives in Somerset with a flying cow and a cat.

Read more about Nicholas's daft family

MY DAD'S GOT AN ALLIGATOR!
MY GRANNY'S GREAT ESCAPE
MY MUM'S GOING TO EXPLODE!
MY BROTHER'S FAMOUS BOTTOM

Are you feeling silly enough to read more?

THE HUNDRED-MILE-AN-HOUR DOG
RETURN OF THE HUNDRED-MILE-AN-HOUR DOG
WANTED! THE HUNDRED-MILE-AN-HOUR DOG

BEWARE! KILLER TOMATOES
CHICKEN SCHOOL
KRAZY KOW SAVES THE WORLD – WELL, ALMOST

LAUGH YOUR SOCKS OFF WITH

Jeremy STRONG

My Dad's Got an Alligator!

Illustrated by

Nick Sharratt

PUFFIN

For the Light and Love in my Life

PUFFIN BOOKS

Published by the Penguin Group
Penguin Books Ltd, 80 Strand, London WC2R ORL, England
Penguin Group (USA) Inc., 375 Hudson Street, New York, New York 10014, USA
Penguin Group (Canada), 90 Eglinton Avenue East, Suite 700, Toronto, Ontario, Canada M4P 2Y3
(a division of Pearson Penguin Canada Inc.)
Penguin Ireland, 25 St Stephen's Green, Dublin 2, Ireland (a division of Penguin Books Ltd)
Penguin Group (Australia), 250 Camberwell Road, Camberwell, Victoria 3124, Australia
(a division of Pearson Australia Group Pty Ltd)
Penguin Books India Pvt Ltd, 11 Community Centre, Panchsheel Park, New Delhi – 110 017, India
Penguin Group (NZ), 67 Apollo Drive, Mairangi Bay, Auckland 1310, New Zealand
(a division of Pearson New Zealand Ltd)
Penguin Books (South Africa) (Pty) Ltd, 24 Sturdee Avenue, Rosebank, Johannesburg 2196, South Africa

Penguin Books Ltd, Registered Offices: 80 Strand, London WC2R ORL, England

penguin.com

First published by Viking 1994
Published in Puffin Books 1996
This edition published 2007

5

Text copyright © Jeremy Strong, 1994
Illustrations copyright © Nick Sharratt, 1994
All rights reserved

The moral right of the author and illustrator has been asserted

Set in Baskerville MT
Made and printed in England by Clays Ltd, St Ives plc

British Library Cataloguing in Publication Data
A CIP catalogue record for this book is available from the British Library

ISBN: 978-0-141-32237-7

Contents

1 Introducing a Vegetarian Alligator

My dad's got an alligator! He brought it
home from work. It used
to belong to this
man at the
paper-mill where
Dad works, but he couldn't
look after it any longer, so Dad said he
would. He's always doing crazy things like
that. He's great.

The alligator is almost as long as our
sofa. Its eyes are black and yellow and they
stare at you all the time. After a while it

made me feel quite
uncomfortable,
as if it thought
I was dinner or
something. Dad said I was being silly. The
alligator couldn't possibly be hungry

because it had just eaten six small children and the crossing patrol man outside the school. I suppose he thought that was funny.

I don't think Mum is very happy about having an alligator in the house. She hates things with lots of teeth. (She can't even bear to look at Granny's falsies when she puts them in cleaning fluid overnight!)

Dad pointed out that people have lots of teeth too. Mum looked at him really sharply and said she could think of some people she didn't much care for sometimes. (Ouch!)

'Well, this alligator is completely harmless,' said Dad. 'In fact, it's a vegetarian.'

'Don't be so stupid, Ronald,' snapped Mum. 'Its teeth are pointed. Sharp, pointed teeth are used for eating meat. What on earth do you think Granny will make of it?'

Dad gave her a tiger-leer. 'What do you think the alligator will make of *Granny*?' he asked. Mum glared back at him. I don't know why, but sometimes my dad just can't see when Mum is actually a bit upset. 'Listen,' Dad went on. 'This alligator has never eaten anyone, never even bitten anyone. Not even a nibble.'

'Oh yes,' Mum retorted. 'And your name is Crocodile Dundee I suppose?' She went straight upstairs to lock herself in the bedroom! I don't know what she's scared of. I think the alligator is adorable. It has this sort of lopsided smile on its face.

Sometimes it closes both eyes
and then opens its jaws very
slowly and very wide. Then all
of a sudden they snap shut.
KERLUNK!
Dad said it would
make a brilliant flycatcher. He's trying to
think of a good name for it, and so am I.

I don't know why we have to worry
about Granny. She spends most of the day
in her room playing pool on the mini
snooker-table Dad gave her last Christmas.
She's almost completely deaf. This is what
happened when I went to tell her about the
alligator:

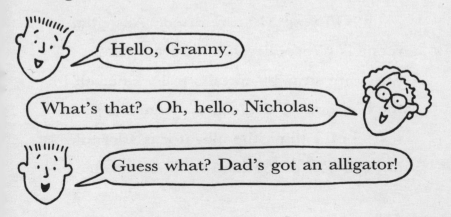

Hello, Granny.

What's that? Oh, hello, Nicholas.

Guess what? Dad's got an alligator!

You want to see Granny later? But you can see me now, dear. I'll just pot the yellow.

No – I said DAD HAS GOT AN ALLIGATOR!

Your father wants to know if I want potato? Is it teatime already? Tell him yes. I always like a bit of boiled potato. Thank you for asking. Oh fiddlesticks, missed!

See what I mean? It's hardly worth the bother. Even so, I hope the alligator doesn't eat her!

2 How to Redecorate Your Kitchen!

Problems. Dad's alligator has eaten two cushions from the sofa. The TV remote control has vanished too. We think that's been swallowed as well, because each time the alligator snaps his jaws shut the TV changes channels.

I want Neighbours

Mum shouted at Dad because he had told her the alligator was harmless. 'It *is* harmless,' insisted Dad. 'It eats cushions. Where's the harm in that? It was only making itself at home.'

'So what's it going to nibble next? The whole sofa? I suppose it ate the TV control so it could watch its favourite TV programme. It's no good, Ron. I am not having it in the house any longer. Have you seen the state of the kitchen?'

'It *likes* dog food.'

'Yes I know, but it doesn't have to puncture the cans with its teeth and then pulverize them. There's dog food squirted all  over the kitchen. It's on the floor. It's on the walls and, believe it or not, Ron, it's on the ceiling. Who's going to clean it up?'

Dad looked desperately at me. I shrugged my shoulders and retreated rapidly. Mum fixed Dad with a razor-sharp glare. '*You're* going to clean it, Ron,' she said in a voice made from pure Toledo steel. 'You!'

I can't wait to see Dad cleaning. He's never cleaned anything in his life. Mum's always complaining about it.

Mum has got one of Granny's old walking-sticks and tied a barbecue fork to the end of it so that she can protect herself. Dad just laughed, which is more than he'll do when he has to clean that kitchen! He's shut the alligator in the garage because he's building a cage for it now, out in the garden. He's using one of the legs from the *Tyrannosaurus rex* for the cage.

I know that sounds odd, but last year Dad had one of his

BRILLIANT IDEAS.

(He gets these about once a week.) He decided he was going to make a slide for me. Then he said he was going to make it in the shape of a *Tyrannosaurus rex*. He got all this wire and wood and built a huge frame in the back garden.

Your hedge is too high!

That drainpipe is the wrong colour!

No bonfires on Sundays!

It looked a bit weird and Mr and Mrs Tugg, the next-door neighbours, complained to the council. Dad doesn't like the Tuggs very much because they always seem to be complaining about something or other. Whenever he sees them marching up the front path he yells, 'The Martians are coming!' Anyhow, the council said they couldn't do anything about it.

Dad never finished the tyrannosaurus. He started covering the head with the fibreglass stuff you use for repairing cars and then he ran out, or just got fed up. The fibreglass head and wire frame is still there. It looks a bit like a vampire horse.

Now the tyrannosaurus has an alligator in one leg. It must be the only tyrannosaurus in the world that can eat things with its left foot!

Dad wants to call the alligator Norman. Talk about boring. Mum grunted

and suggested we call it Armageddon, which
I didn't understand. Dad said it meant The
End of the World and Life As We Know It.
I still didn't understand
why it should be a
good name for an
alligator and Dad said
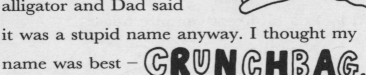
it was a stupid name anyway. I thought my
name was best – **CRUNCHBAG.**

'That's exactly what I was thinking,'
grinned Dad. 'Crunchbag is a brilliant
name. I'm glad I thought of it.'

'But *I* said it!' I shouted.

'Ah, but I was thinking it,' said Dad.

♪ ♭ ♪ ∠ # 3 Singsong Time ♪ ♪ ♫

The trouble with my dad is that when he
thinks he's done something clever he goes
all stupid and starts singing. I don't mean
like normal people sing. On no. Nothing my
dad does is normal. He's got this karaoke
machine and a microphone and amplifiers.

You could hear him on Mars.

As soon as he'd finished
the cage he was upstairs
warbling. I could hear Mum
hammering on the door. She was probably
telling him to shut up, but he wouldn't have

been able to hear
her. He was making
too much noise.
Even Crunchbag
seemed to be trying
to bury his head in
the ground.

I went to see if Granny was all right, with such a din going on. I asked if she was OK and she said, 'Yes, dear. It's in the top drawer under my karate tunic.' Don't ask me what she was talking about. I just shut the door quietly and went into the front room. That was when I saw Mr Tugg charging up our path. He didn't look very happy.

What a row! When Dad realized who was at the front door he started singing 'The Martians are coming, hurrah! hurrah!' Mr Tugg shouted at Mum, complaining about the racket that was going on. Mum said Dad was only singing.

'You call that singing?' squeaked Mr Tugg. (Nobody squeaks quite like Mr Tugg. He sounds like a balloon when you pinch the neck and let the air out slowly.) His moustache was jumping about like a caterpillar with a heart attack. Mr Tugg is ever so little, even shorter than Mum. He's bald in the middle of his head but he tries to camouflage it by combing straggly bits over the top. It looks utterly stupid. I'll never do anything like that if *I* go bald.

Eventually Mum went to the fuse-box and switched all the electricity off. It was the only way to stop Dad's karaoke machine. After that, he came downstairs.

'Evening, Mr Tugg,' he said. 'What a fine night for a moonlit stroll with a

beautiful woman on your arm!' and he slipped one arm through Mum's.

'That singing...' began Mr Tugg.

'Ah, you like it then,' Dad said quickly. (He can be a real stirrer!) 'Yes, I was in fine form tonight.' And he started

again on the doorstep. 'Just a song at
twilight…'

Mr Tugg left very quickly. You
could almost see the anger
spitting out of him like mini
lightning bolts. It was a good
thing he didn't know about
Crunchbag. (The alligator was by
this time buried under an Everest of mud.)

Mum wasn't very pleased though. She
said it was all right for Dad, larking about
and enjoying himself, but that kind of
behaviour upset some people.
'They take life more seriously,'
she added. Dad went down on
one knee and clasped
his hands together.
Guess what he started singing? 'Daisy,
Daisy, give me your answer, do…'

Mum couldn't help smiling. I'm sure I
heard her call Mr Tugg a 'goblin'!

Granny was calling from her room, so I went to see if she was OK. She was sitting in front of the television watching a blank screen. She asked me to sort out the sound for her.

'But Granny, there isn't any picture either,' I said.

'I think it's foggy,' said Granny.

'Mum switched off the electricity,' I shouted. 'The TV isn't on.'

'No thank you, Nicholas. I had a cup of tea not ten minutes ago.' Sometimes I look at Granny and realize why Dad's the way he is. After all, she is his mother.

4 A Wolf at the Door

AWHOOO!

Mum and Dad have been arguing again. I don't believe it. Last night they were all lovey-dovey and went for a smoochy walk. But this morning it was as if the fifth ice-age had suddenly begun.

YUK!

Mum couldn't find the chicken she had bought for Sunday lunch. She knew she had put it in the fridge, but the fridge was chicken-less. How mysterious! What could possibly have happened to the poor little Sunday chicken? Who could possibly have eaten it? Go on, guess.

Of course, Mum knew all along. There was only one possible suspect, and his

name had nine letters, beginning with a C. The real mystery was that there was no way Crunchbag could have opened the fridge by himself. For one thing he was still stuck inside the tyrannosaurus's left leg. Besides, how would an alligator get into a fridge? With a tin-opener? A crowbar? A nice little lump of plastic explosive? I could see Mum going through all the possibilities in her head. She had that Miss Marple look on her face. Finally she looked straight at Dad.

'*You* gave that chicken to Crunchbag, didn't you?'

'Me?' squeaked Dad. He's hopeless when he's telling lies. He looked across at me with huge innocent eyes. 'How can you possibly suspect such a thing?'

Mum sighed. 'Ronald, it's written all over your face. It's no use denying it. Crunchbag didn't take the chicken, and

`I did it!`

Nicholas certainly didn't. For Heaven's sake, that was our Sunday lunch. How could you do such a thing?'

Dad shrugged. 'I didn't want Crunchbag to starve. That would have been cruelty to animals.'

'And what about cruelty to poor human beings who have to go without their Sunday lunch?' demanded Mum. 'That beast will have to go!'

I think Dad made a bad mistake then. He laughed. Mum threw the mushrooms at him and went storming off to the kitchen. Dad looked at me, pulled a wry face and shrugged again. 'What can you do?' he said. 'What *can* you do?'

I know how Mum feels sometimes. My dad can make you laugh so much you think you'll die, but it's a horrible feeling when you can't help laughing and you know you shouldn't because actually there's something serious happening.

Mum and I had omelettes for lunch, without mushrooms. Dad didn't have anything. He prowled up and down outside the dining-room. Then he started howling like a hungry wolf. **AWHOOOO!** Mum slammed the door and glared so hard at me I didn't even dare smile. When she was watching telly later I managed to sneak Dad a sandwich.

Psst! Peanut-butter sarnie!

5 Kiss-and-make-up Time

Mum was very quiet and thoughtful this morning. In the middle of lunch she suddenly turned to me. 'Why did I marry your father?' she asked. I hadn't got a clue!

'Was he like this when you first met him?' I asked. Mum smiled and looked dreamily out of the window.

'I suppose so. I suppose I was a bit daft too – in those days. I must have been daft because I married him.'

'Curried jam?' Granny squawked suddenly. 'No, dear, you can't get curried jam anywhere these days.'

Mum patted Granny's hand, winked at me and then sighed fondly. 'I think I loved him for his beard,' she murmured. His beard!

How can you love someone for their beard?

When Dad got home from work he had brought Mum a present. He put it on the dining-room table, all wrapped up in pretty paper. I tried to think what it could be but it was such a weird shape. When Mum opened it she found a ready-roast chicken.

She (KISSED) him! She even said she was sorry she hadn't given him any Sunday lunch. Dad said it didn't matter because I had sneaked him a peanut-butter sandwich. So much for *that* secret. You can't trust anyone. Luckily Mum didn't seem to mind.

They've made up again. Sometimes I just can't believe those two. What am I supposed to do now? I want to die. THEY HAVE BOTH STARTED SINGING ON DAD'S KARAOKE MACHINE! I think I'll go downstairs and play snooker with Granny. She's certain to beat me, but to have a conversation with her might take my mind off my embarrassing parents. Perhaps I shall leave home.

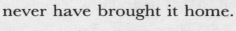

6 The Deep-pond Diver

The doorbell rang at half-past six this morning! It was Mr Tugg, the Martian from next door. He was amazingly calm, at least to start with. He wanted to know if we would like our alligator back because it was in their garden. In fact, it was cruising about their goldfish pond.

Mum's eyes were on fire. She bellowed up the stairs at Dad. It was all his fault. She said she knew that Dad should

never have brought it home. Dad came rushing down in his dressing-gown. 'Just a moment,' he said to Mr Tugg. 'How do you know it's *our* alligator?'

Good question, Dad! Mr Tugg didn't think so though. He began to do one of his

23

very-loud-firework impressions.

'This is the only house in
the street with a pet
alligator!' he fizzed. 'It's
probably the only house
in the *country* with a pet
alligator. Of course it's yours.

Don't think I haven't seen it from over the
fence, making a pig of itself with cans of
dog food.'

Dad folded his
arms. 'Making a pig of
itself, Mr Tugg? How
can an alligator make
itself into a pig? What an extraordinary
creature!'

'Don't bandy clever words with me!'
crackled Mr Tugg. 'The alligator is yours. If
you don't come and remove it at once I
shall call the police!' Mr Tugg fizzled off
down the garden path.

My dad doesn't take anything seriously, except making jokes. He's a dedicated joker. There are times when I wish the ground would swallow me up or I lived on another planet. He went back inside the house and came back wearing flippers on his feet and goggles and a snorkel on his face.

He flip-flopped into the Tuggs' garden. Mr Tugg was speechless. Dad waved at him, held his nose, and waded into the garden pond singing 'We all live in a yellow submarine...'

Crunchbag is not terribly big, but he is very wriggly and strong. His tail can be really wicked. He knocked Dad

over five times.
It was a real
wrestling match,
like Tarzan, except
Tarzan doesn't

wear pyjamas. (Or goggles, or flippers, or a
snorkel...)

I cheered, but Mr Tugg looked at me
so coldly I felt as if an iceberg had just

fallen on me. We
hauled Crunchbag
back to our house,
leaving Mr Tugg
crouched over his

pond, staring into the depths. I don't think
there are any goldfish left.

7 Bubble Bath

Dad reckons Crunchbag is desperate for water and that was why he chewed his way out of the tyrannosaurus leg. Mum told him he would have to sort out something better for Crunchbag or she would leave home. She said her suitcase was all ready. 'All I have to do is pack it.'

Dad told her not to worry. He's always saying that. It didn't work anyway, because half an hour later there was a blood-curdling scream from the bathroom.

THERE'S AN ALLIGATOR
IN MY BATH!

Mum stood at the top of the stairs, wrapped in a towel and howling. 'Ronald! How could you! I was just about to get into the water when I saw this massive pair of jaws

opening. IT WAS SMILING AT ME!' she
screamed. 'Get it out, Ron; out, out, out!'

She actually hit Dad with her face-
flannel. Crunchbag lay in the bath and
watched all this with his yellow slitty eyes.

Then he ate all the soap and my plastic
boat. Mum was so upset she had a drink of
brandy, and then another.

'I only put him there to keep him out
of mischief,' explained Dad.

'Mischief!' Mum almost choked on
her brandy. 'Putting him in *my* bath is
keeping him out of mischief?'

'I'm sorting out a new cage for him. I
had to put him somewhere. Besides,

Crunchbag needs water.'

'Oh yes, and I suppose he needed all the Tuggs' goldfish too?' cried Mum. 'He ate fifteen prize goldfish this morning! It's not good enough, Ron, I won't have any more of this. Look at him – he's a monster! Either he goes, or I do!'

All eyes turned to Crunchbag in the bath. Large soapy bubbles were coming out of the side of his mouth. He was wearing that silly grin of his. 'I bet his teeth are nice and clean,' said Dad.

8 Anyone for a Picnic?

Mum is never cross with Dad for long. I think things are exciting when Dad is around and Mum likes the excitement – like today. We went for a picnic. Dad said that Crunchbag must have water and, since Mum didn't like sharing her bath with an alligator, Dad thought we could drive down to a river and have a picnic at the same time.

'But where are we going?' asked Mum.

'Down to Shoreham village. There's a good shallow river there. Nicholas can paddle about if he wants and there are plenty of fields where we can picnic. The sun's shining. It will be great.'

I thought it sounded wonderful. Mum gazed out of the window. She was watching Crunchbag roaming round his new cage.

'I'm not sharing the car with Mega-Jaws out there.'

'No problem,' said Dad. 'Leave it to me.'

We took the picnic-box outside. Dad was standing by the car. 'Ta-ra!' he shouted, stepping back. He had just finished tying Crunchbag to the roof-rack! He did a

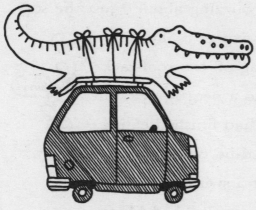

little song and dance: 'I'm a clever chappie, and I'm very happy; There's a 'gator on the roof and I'm telling you the troof...'

Mum got into the car, keeping a careful eye on Crunchbag, and off we went. Shoreham isn't far from where we live.

We found a field by the river and sat down with the picnic. It was very peaceful.

There was a field of cows chewing the grass on the opposite bank, and bees buzzing about — just the sort of thing you'd expect really. Dad took Crunchbag off the roof-rack and tied him to a nearby tree, but as soon as we had finished eating, Dad announced he was going to take Crunchbag for a swim.

'Are you sure?' asked Mum.

'He'll love it,' Dad said, tying a long piece of rope round Crunchbag's neck. He led the alligator down to the water.

Love it? Crunchbag went bonkers over it! He loved it so much he went zooming off

at hyper-speed, towing Dad behind. For just
a few seconds Dad managed to keep up,
then he fell flat on his face by the riverbank.

Dad's yells turned to spluttering
gurgles as Crunchbag trawled Dad through
the river. It wasn't a deep river, but it was a
wet river, full of straggly waterweed. They

came out on the muddy bank on the far
side. It was at that point that Dad finally
gave up and let go of the rope.

9 Stop That Alligator!

Crunchbag went wandering off into the
cows' field, leaving Dad face-down in river-
gunge. It might have been all right if there
hadn't been any cows in the field. I don't
know if Crunchbag was hungry or if he was
simply interested.

The cows took one look at this

alligator clomping towards
them and then there was this
sort of cow-explosion, with
cows mooing and

bellowing and leaping about all
over the place. Crunchbag was
right there in the middle, with
his jaws going snip-snap.

Dad struggled to his feet like

some monster from the deep, festooned with slimy weed, and started squelching around trying to calm all the cows down. Mum stood on our side of the river and screamed.

'Stop them, Ronald! Stop them before all their milk curdles!'

 Then the farmer appeared with a shotgun! He roared at Dad, telling him to 'keep that pesky dog under control'.

DOG!? He must have been blind! Dad threw himself on Crunchbag and they had another of those massive Tarzan fights, which Dad eventually won. Unfortunately he was not only covered in river muck by this time, but also some rather unpleasant stuff that you get in cow-fields.

The farmer was speechless as he watched Dad wade back across the river towing an alligator. He started running back

to the farmhouse. I suppose he wanted
witnesses.

Dad lashed Crunchbag to the roof-
rack. 'Get in,' he growled. 'We're going
home.'

'Just a moment,' said Mum. 'You're
not sitting in the car in that state. Look at
you! You pong to high heaven. You can sit
in the boot and I shall drive.'

Dad didn't believe her. I did. She
opened the boot and Dad had to climb in
and sit there. She was quite right. He was a
stink-bomb. Mum and I got in the car and
she drove home.

Halfway home we heard a police siren
getting louder and louder. I looked behind
and saw a police car coming up behind us
at top speed.
It wasn't us
they were
after because

we weren't doing anything wrong. Mum slowed down to let them pass. They went squealing ahead of us, lights flashing, and immediately pulled us over. Us! Mum stopped the car and we watched one of the police officers slowly get out of his car. He pulled down his helmet, straightened his tie, tugged both sleeves neatly, got out his notebook and sauntered over to us.

 I'm sorry to bother you, madam, but did you know that there is a crocodile strapped to your roof?

It's not a crocodile, officer, it's an alligator. We have just taken him to the river for a bath.

 I see, madam. And did you know that there is a tramp sitting in the boot of your car?

He's not a tramp, officer, he's my husband. I am taking him for a bath too.

The policeman started to write all this down, then gave up in despair. He tore out the page and waved us on. I suppose he thought nobody would believe him — like the farmer. Quite right too. After all, how many people take their pet alligator swimming in the local river?

10 Hunt the Granny

Crunchbag escaped again last night. I never knew alligators could dig tunnels. He's been really busy.

There are piles of earth everywhere.

Dad was at work when we discovered he was missing. Mum got into a right panic. She rushed back indoors and got the walking-stick with the barbecue fork on the end. I don't know how she thinks she's going to defend herself with that!

She set about poking and prodding the bushes, but she couldn't find him. She sent me to make sure that Granny was all right. 'Shut her door tight,' Mum warned. 'We don't want her having a heart attack because she's had an alligator trying to get into her bed.'

I went off to Granny, and guess what?

SHE WASN'T THERE!

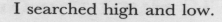

I searched high and low.

I even looked in the 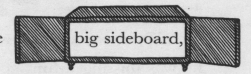 big sideboard,

but what Granny would have been doing in there I don't know. I reported back and gave Mum the news.

Talk about hysterics! She threw her hands up in the air and dashed into the house screaming, 'Mother! Mother! Where are you?' She looked in all the places I had already thought of, but there was no doubt that we were Granny-less.

 Mum came downstairs very slowly, her face like a dentist's patient. She stared at me with

huge eyes. 'She's been eaten. It's that alligator. I know it's that alligator, Nicholas! Dad should never have brought it into the house. Crunchbag has escaped and he's eaten Granny. He must have smelt her.'

I suppose he could have smelt her because Granny whiffs strongly of Tandoori Chicken Tikka, which is her most favourite meal of all time.

'Surely there'd be blood somewhere, or bits of clothing,' I suggested. Mum held out one hand. She was holding Granny's spectacles. One of the arms was twisted and broken.

I still thought there ought to be some blood somewhere. 'I mean, you can't chew up a whole person without blood squirting out a bit, can you?' I said helpfully. Mum clutched at the stairs.

'Don't say such awful things!' she cried. 'It's your granny we're talking about.'

Mum decided to telephone the police. 'We can't have a man-eating alligator roaming the streets,' she said. I pointed out that it wasn't a man-eater, it was a granny-eater. I wish I hadn't. Mum turned on me, almost in tears.

'That's right, make a joke of it just like your father! This is serious, Nicholas, serious!'

I suppose she was right. She picked up the phone and was just dialling, when Granny walked in through the front door. Mum just about fainted. The phone fell from her fingers. At last a small, broken voice came from her throat. 'Are you a ghost?'

'Burning toast?' Granny said, sniffing the air. 'No, I can't smell any burning toast, can you, Nicholas?'

'No, Granny,' I smiled, hugging her. Mum came to

life and rushed over. She was all over
Granny. She kept hugging and touching her
to make sure she was real. 'Where have you
been? I was so worried.'

'Yes, dear, I think it's going to rain.
You can put me down now.'

Mum and I looked at each other. I
shook my head and muttered 'deaf as a
doorpost' to Mum. Then she saw Granny's
shopping bag. There was a video in it,

 So that was where she
had been – up to the
video shop! At least she's
been found, which is more
than I can say about Crunchbag. He's still
out there somewhere.

11 A Ride on the Wild Side

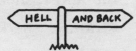

Boy oh boy! The Martians from next door were in a jumbo rage today. Mr Tugg has been charging round like a rogue elephant half the afternoon. I even heard Mrs Tugg mutter 'it's awful' at one point, which is truly amazing because I have never heard her speak before today. (This is probably because Mr Tugg says enough for ten people at once.)

The first warning we had was from Dad. 'The Martians are coming! Quick, fetch me my catapult...'

Man the guns! Get to the battlements!

As soon as Dad opened the front door Mr Tugg seized him furiously by one arm and began dragging him down the path.

44

'Look!' he bellowed. 'Just come and look!'

'I am looking,' panted Dad. 'Is this a game of I Spy?'

Mr Tugg stopped instantly and glared so closely into Dad's face that Dad had to lean backwards to avoid being stabbed by Mr Tugg's beaky nose. 'Don't you dare make jokes about this! This is it! It's the end! I've had enough, do you hear? Enough!'

Dad tried to calm him down. 'I can see you're a bit upset, Mr Tugg.'

This made things even worse. For a  few seconds Mr Tugg was speechless. You could see the volcanic explosion struggling to reach the surface of his face. Then he erupted.

'Upset? I'm fuming! I'm furious! I'm

livid!' His arms were going up and down and he was walking round and round in small circles.

'But just what is the matter?' asked Dad.

'Follow me,' commanded Mr Tugg, and he led the way round to his house.

Parked outside was a Road Rescue van. The Tuggs' car was strapped on the back. It's one of those three-wheeler things. It looked rumpled, crumpled and sad. It was covered in dirt and bits of plants. The

front end looked as if it had been a very bad loser in a boxing match.

'Oh dear,' said Dad. 'You *have* had an accident. I hope no one was hurt?'

'My car's been hurt!' wailed Mr Tugg. 'It's a wreck, a write-off. And do you know *why* my car looks like...like...like...this?'

'I don't know, Mr Tugg, but I have a feeling that you are going to tell me.'

Mr Tugg eyed Dad as if he wasn't sure if he was being laughed at or not. He tried to smooth his few extra-long hairs back over his bald patch.

'This morning Mrs Tugg and I decided we would go for a drive in the country.'

'Nice day for it,' agreed Dad.

'Yes, it was a nice day and off we went. The sun was shining...'

'It still is,' Dad pointed out cheerfully.

'Don't interrupt!' bawled Mr Tugg. 'This is *my* story!'

'Sorry,' Dad murmured.

'The sun was shining. We were travelling down this lovely country lane. I looked out on one side and saw birds singing in the bushes. I looked out on the other side and saw butterflies fluttering about. I looked in my rear-view mirror. And what do you think I saw?' Mr Tugg paused dramatically.

Tweet

Tweet

Flutter

Flutter

'A squashed hedgehog?' suggested Dad.

'I SAW AN ALLIGATOR! THERE WAS AN ALLIGATOR SITTING IN THE BACK OF MY CAR! ITS TEETH WERE THIS CLOSE TO MY HEAD! ITS JAWS WERE WIDE OPEN!'

Mum's hands flew to her face. 'Oh, Mr Tugg! What *did* you do?'

'I DROVE OFF THE ROAD!' screamed Mr Tugg, pointing at his three-wheeler. 'I went through a hedge and hit a tree!'

For the first time, Dad actually looked really worried and he clutched Mr Tugg's arm. 'But what about Crunchbag? Is he all right?'

'I don't know,' Mr Tugg answered with dangerous calm, then exploded once more. 'Look at my beautiful car!' He ran to the three-wheeler and hit it with his fists. A wing mirror fell off. 'Look at it! It's a wreck! My lovely car!'

Dad was already getting Mum's mountain bike out of the garage. 'I must go and find Crunchbag. He may be hurt. Don't worry about the car, Mr Tugg. The insurance company will cover the damage.'

Crunchbag! Crunchbag!

And before anyone could say anything else Dad had wobbled off down the road pedalling furiously and shouting, 'Crunchbag! Crunchbag!' at the top of his voice.

That left poor Mum (and myself!) to cope with Mr and Mrs Tugg. I don't know how she managed it. She does have to put up with a lot. The last thing we wanted to deal with was the next-door Martians, but she did. She made a pot of tea and got them calmed down. They went away peacefully enough, but Mum's done in. She just collapsed into an armchair and stared straight ahead. I'm sure she muttered something about becoming a nun. I don't know what to do to help.

peace and quiet at last!

And what about Crunchbag? I wonder if he's all right? The Tuggs had seatbelts on,  so they were OK, but cars don't have seatbelts for alligators. He may be injured. I think I'll make Mum a cup of tea. Maybe I'll have one myself. On the other hand perhaps I'll just help Mum pack her suitcase. I think I might join her. Can nuns keep their sons?

12 The Mad Cyclist

Crunchbag has been missing for three days
and Mum seems to have recovered
completely. It's weird, because
all the time Crunchbag was
here she was nervous and
worried, while Dad was all
jokey and cheerful. Now it's
the other way round. Mum
has started using Dad's
karaoke machine. She's got a
better voice than Dad. I
almost feel like joining in.

I am sailing, ♪ I am sailing...!

I've hardly seen Dad. He spends
all his spare time riding round
the neighbourhood on his bike
shouting for the alligator.
One of the ladies from
further up the road came
round yesterday to ask if

Oh, Crunchbag!

Dad was all right. She thought maybe he'd had a funny turn – you know, gone a bit dippy in the head. Mum smiled and said that wasn't anything new. He'd been like that for ages. It's quite a relief to see her back to her usual self. She doesn't worry about Crunchbag at all, but I do. I wish I knew that he was OK.

13 Under Lock and Key

You won't believe what's happened in the last two hours! First of all Dad came rocketing down the road on his bike at turbo-speed, chased by a police car. The lights were flashing and the siren was so loud you would have thought he had just stolen the crown jewels.

Oi, come back!

Puff Puff

POLICE

Everyone came rushing out of their houses to see what was going on. Mum came in from the garden and was just betting me a million pounds that all the noise was something to do with Dad, when he burst into the house, shouting at her.

'They're after me! They're after me! They want to put me away! Quick!' He threw himself into the cupboard under the stairs and pulled the door shut.

Then the police car stopped on our driveway. Two policemen got out, raced straight into the house and just about pushed Mum and me up against the hall wall. One burst into the back room, yelling and waving his truncheon, much to Granny's surprise. The other one asked Mum if she was OK.

'Of course I'm all right. What on earth is going on?'

'We've just seen a madman come running into this house, madam! We've got to catch him. He's quite desperate. He cycled up your garden path – probably a stolen bicycle I shouldn't wonder. It's a ladies' mountain bike. What kind of man would ride a ladies' bicycle I ask you? He's been terrorizing the area for days, racing round and screaming 'CRUNCHBAG!' at old-age pensioners and little kiddies. We've got to get him before he becomes even more dangerous.'

I could see Mum was desperately trying not to laugh. But it was no use. She suddenly collapsed in a fit of giggles, and so did I. She looked at me and laughed even more. I could hardly hold myself together I was laughing so much.

The two policemen were getting quite cross, but we couldn't stop, not for ages. Eventually Mum managed to blurt out the whole story about Dad and the alligator. The police were clearly disappointed. 'Looks like we've been on a wild-goose chase,' said one. Mum clutched his arm.

'It isn't a wild goose, it's a wild alligator!' she giggled.

The police left in a nasty huff, saying
that people who wasted police time ought to
be locked up.

Anyhow, to finish off, Dad started
shouting from the cupboard under the
stairs. He wanted to be let out now that the
police had gone. Mum stopped laughing
and stood outside the little door
listening to Dad. She looked
across at me and gave a long,
satisfied sigh. 'I think it's
high time we took
control of your
father, don't you,
Nicky? Maybe those
two policemen were
right.' I nodded, although I had no idea
what she was planning to do next.

She got the key for the cupboard and
locked Dad inside! 'I'm leaving you in there,
you horrible man!' she shouted through the

keyhole. 'You're a dangerous madman and it's the only safe place for people who keep their alligators in their gardens. Goodnight!'

That was two hours ago. Dad isn't shouting so much now. I don't know how long Mum is going to leave him there. I can't even sneak him some food. Mum's got the only key.

14 A Night Under the Stairs

Granny got us up at two o'clock this morning ! Well, actually I suppose it was Dad's fault really. All his shouting woke her up. It woke me up too. By the time I got to the top of the stairs Granny was down there talking to the cupboard.

'Is there anyone there?'

'Oh, thank goodness,' came Dad's muffled voice. 'Who's out there? Is that you, Nicky?'

Granny put one ear to the keyhole. 'Is anyone there?' she said again.

'Yes! I'm here!' yelled Dad. 'Let me out at once!'

'You'll have to speak louder,' Granny shouted

through the keyhole. 'Stop whispering.'

'LET ME OUT!' screamed Dad. Granny stepped back a pace, grimly muttering to herself. 'There's somebody in that cupboard. I'll soon sort him out!' She hurried back to her room and fetched a snooker cue. She stood by the door and raised the stick with both hands. 'Come out at once,' she commanded. 'I shall knock your head off!'

Mum came hurrying out of the bedroom pulling on her dressing-gown. She stood next to me, leaning over the banister and watching the little drama downstairs. She grabbed my hand and squeezed it. I'm sure she was enjoying every minute.

'Come out, you beastly thief!' shouted Granny.

'I can't come out, you steaming

bumblehead! It's me, Mother! Your son, Ron!'

'That sounds like my son, Ron,' muttered Granny, gripping her cue even more firmly. 'The sneaky stinker is trying to fool me. I'll soon teach him!' There was a resounding **THWACK!** as Granny hit the door with her stick. 'Take that!' she cried. 'And that!'

Mum whispered in my ear, 'I think I'd better sort this out.' She went downstairs.

'There's a man in your cupboard, dear,' declared Granny.

'I know. Don't worry,' Mum shouted into Granny's hearing-aid. 'I'll call the police. You go back to bed and get some sleep.'

'You should call the police,' advised Granny. 'I'm going back to bed to get some sleep.' And off she went. Meanwhile the cupboard door was being shaken almost off its hinges.

'Is that you, Brenda? For pity's sake let me out. Please!'

Mum looked up at me. 'Shall I?' she whispered, bending down by the door. Before I could answer she straightened up. 'No, how stupid of me to even consider it. Come on, Nicholas, we should all be in bed fast asleep. There's no point wasting time over *lunatics* who have *no consideration* for others and insist on keeping *alligators*!' Her teeth snapped shut on the last word, just like Crunchbag. I took one last glance at the cupboard and we went back to bed.

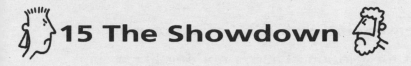

15 The Showdown

Dad spent the whole night under the stairs! Mum went down to the kitchen and made breakfast very noisily, so that Dad could hear everything. She clattered breakfast plates just outside the cupboard door. She had this wonderful serene look on her face, as if she was completely at peace. She was certainly completely in charge.

Meanwhile Dad was shouting from behind the door, 'What's all that noise? What are you doing out there?'

Mum stood by the door and winked at me. 'I'm having my breakfast, you nasty madman. I'm stirring my coffee. Hmm! It smells delicious!'

'Let me out, Brenda, please. I'll do anything...'

'I'm buttering my hot toast and piling on the marmalade. Listen to it crunch between my teeth. Oh, what a magnificent taste-explosion. There's nothing like a slap-up breakfast first thing in the morning.'

'LET ME OUT!' screamed Dad, attacking the door again.

Mum stopped play-acting and bent down beside the door. 'Do you promise to put away your clothes instead of leaving them lying about all over the place?'

'YES!'

'Do you promise to clean the bath after you've used it?'

'YES!'

'Do you promise to clean the toilet?'

'NO!'

'Wrong answer!' snapped Mum. 'Someone has to clean it.'

'All right, yes, anything, but let me out!'

'Just one small point, Ronald,' said
Mum in an icy tone. 'Do you promise to
get rid of that alligator?'

Bye-bye!

'YES! YES! YES!'
cried Dad.

Mum opened the door.

Dad was so stiff he had to crawl out
on his hands and knees. The look on his
face was like a cardboard
box that had been out in
the rain all night...
completely crumpled.

Mum ran him a huge hot bath so that
he could relax and unstiffen. Then she
made him a giant's breakfast — fried egg,
toast, sausages, mushrooms, bacon, the lot.

You would have thought he'd been in that cupboard for a month. Sometimes Mum sends me to my room for hours, but she never cooks *me* anything like that when I'm allowed out. It's not fair.

Dad didn't say a word to Mum, but sat there with a gigantic scowl on his face. It wasn't a murderous scowl; it was the face of defeat. I had never seen Dad like it before and I wasn't sure what it meant. He had promised to get rid of Crunchbag, but I couldn't see Dad giving up his alligator without some sort of struggle. Whatever he intended to do there was still one big problem — how do you get rid of something you haven't got? Crunchbag was still out there somewhere.

16 Panic in the Park

Dad spent his whole morning sitting in an armchair, staring at nothing. Mum made him lunch and he still didn't say a word. He wouldn't even talk to me. I was just beginning to get quite worried by his behaviour, when he sprang from the chair, raced to the front window and flung it wide open.

In the far distance I could hear the wail of a siren. It grew steadily louder until a fire-engine went booming past. Hardly had it squealed round the corner when another siren came up fast and a second engine thundered down the road. Several streets away we could hear a police car wailing, approaching from a different direction.

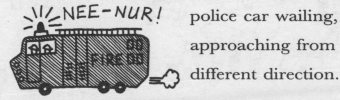

But where were
they all going?

'The park!'
Dad cried. 'Quick – sound the alarm! Tell
the Queen! Call out the army!'

'But, Dad, what's going on?'

He gave me a mad grin. 'I'm going to
save the world, Nicky!' And with that he
leaped out of the front window and went
charging off. What could I do except leap
after him and try to keep up?

'But what's going on, Dad?' I panted from way behind. His answer was a single word flung back over one shoulder.

'CRUNCHBAG!'

Of course! There was a small lake in the park, just right for a water-loving alligator. When we got there it was already surrounded by jostling people and vehicles. There were five fire-engines, eight police cars and two ambulances. There was also an ice-cream van, but I don't think that was

really part of it.

Dad pushed his way down to the lakeside. Out in the centre ducks were thrashing about making a tremendous clatter. Wherever they landed the water would suddenly boil up and the ducks would give strangled squawks and desperately struggle off somewhere else.

The firemen and police had launched a couple of rowing-boats and were paddling about trying to keep up with the ducks. I asked Dad what they were trying to do.

'It's Crunchbag. He's out here!' said Dad with immense satisfaction. 'He's after those ducks. I saw his slitty eyes just now. Well, your time has come, Crunchbag. Superman is on his way!'

The only boats left were pedalos. Dad grabbed one and started pedalling furiously across the lake. The police yelled at him to go back, but he ignored them. 'That's my alligator you're after! I'll deal with him. He is completely in my command – does anything I say.' I don't know why Dad told them such complete rubbish, but the next bit was even worse. He started shouting things like, 'Good Crunchie – Sit! Stay!'

Two of the policemen on the shore gave each other knowing looks. 'That's the mad loony we were after yesterday,' they declared, promptly jumped on another pedalo, and set off in pursuit of Dad.

'Hey! You! You're wanted for questioning! Come here!' The police pedalo was

catching up on Dad and then one of the rowing-boats

joined the chase too. I could hardly bear to watch. The crowd were shouting, the police were bawling through megaphones, Dad was yelling 'Sit! Good Crunchie!' and Crunchbag carried on trying to see how many ducks he could catch in one go.

Dad stopped in the middle of the lake. 'That's right, sir,' bellowed the police. 'Just stay there nice and easy. You'll be all right.' The boats closed in. Dad got to his feet. He tore off his shirt. The crowd cheered. He

Arrrrrr - ar- ar- ar- aarrr!

kicked off his shoes and with a magnificent Tarzan yodel he dived into the lake, throwing himself on top of the cruising alligator.

'He's trying to kill himself!' cried the police, and three of them jumped in after him. The fire brigade didn't want to be left out, so four of them leaped in, with their helmets still on. The crowd began to shout things like 'Spoilsports! Let him fight the alligator. He's a hero!'

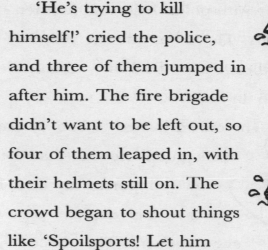

'He's a nutcase!' the police yelled back.

In the middle of the lake there was a tremendous battle going on. First we saw Dad, then we saw Crunchbag, then a few firemen – or was it policemen? They all look the same when they're wet through. There were blue and yellow helmets bobbing about on the water. At last we

heard a yell of 'One, two, three, heave!' and
they pushed Crunchbag into a boat, tied to
an oar with police belts and firemen's
trousers. There was another yell, and this
time they heaved Dad into a boat. He was
tied to an oar too.

The crowd started to boo. It was
really good knowing that the
crowd supported my dad. I
guess he'd given them pretty good
entertainment. The police
on shore had to hold back the
people as Crunchbag and Dad were
brought from the boats. Half the firemen
didn't have any trousers and the police kept
clutching at theirs to stop them falling down
round their ankles.

Boooo!

Leave him alone!

Killjoys!

Boooo!

Dad hung upside down from the oar. He grinned at me as he was carried past. 'Tell them to go easy on the sage and onion stuffing,' he said, just before he was shoved into the back of a police van.

The last I saw of him he was singing cheerfully from behind locked doors as the van was being driven away.

17 Please Release Me!

I raced back to the house and burst in. 'Dad's going to prison!' I yelled at Mum, trying to explain everything and pulling her back out of the house and down the front path.

'This has gone too far,' said Mum. 'It's all right for your father to act daft – everyone expects it these days – but when the police start behaving so childishly something must be done. Come on, Nicholas, we're going to sort this out once and for all.'

I felt an ocean of relief swell into my heart. Mum was taking charge, and she proved to be brilliant. She marched into the

police station and asked for her husband
back, as if he was a ball she'd lost over the
fence.

'And who is your husband, madam?'
asked the desk sergeant.

'The one singing "PLEASE
RELEASE ME, LET ME GO..."'

'I'm sorry, madam, but he's mad and
dangerous.'

'Nonsense! He's over forty, that's all.
Men go like that, you know.' She glared at

the sergeant. 'As far as I know he hasn't actually broken the law, has he?'

The sergeant scratched his head. 'He threw himself in the lake,' he muttered.

'Is that against the law?'

'No, madam, but then he wrestled with that alligator we've got roped up over there.' For the first time I caught sight of Crunchbag,

lurking in the corner with his eyes looking very slitty indeed.

'Is it against the law to wrestle alligators?' asked Mum.

'No, madam.'

'In that case, please let him out and I shall take him home — unless you wish him to carry on singing?'

That clinched it. Dad was brought up from the interview room. He took one look at Mum, threw his arms wide and ran

towards her.

Mum stepped back quickly. 'Don't touch me. You're soggy and horrible. You can get in the boot again and don't say a word.'

The desk sergeant undid Crunchbag's rope and handed the lead over to Dad. Mum snatched it from his hand, let it drop to the floor and delivered her crunch-line.

'Oh, do keep the alligator. He won't be needing it any longer.'

I think Crunchbag agreed, because at this point he fastened both jaws round a big metal waste-paper bin standing in the corner. The last we saw of Crunchbag, there were two policemen trying to prise his jaws open, another one holding his tail and the desk sergeant trying to get his arms around

Crunchbag's body.

'We'll give him to the zoo, madam,' panted the sergeant as he was thrown back against the wall.

Meanwhile Crunchbag was giving the bin a good old shaking and was gaily sprinkling rubbish over most of the lobby.

18 A Toast to Crunchbag

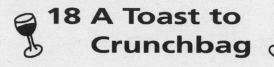

Mum cooked a special meal to celebrate
Crunchbag's departure. We even had wine!
'Here's a toast to our absent alligator

friend,' said Mum,
raising her glass.

'What's that
about an alligator,
dear?' Granny asked.
We burst out laughing.
None of us could
explain of course.
Where would we start?
I'm a bit sad
about Crunchbag going. I think
Dad is too. He was really good
fun while we had him. I've got a
strong feeling that he enjoyed

himself too. I hope he's gone to a good home. Maybe he'll escape and make his way back here...

Guess what we all did after supper? We all sang on Dad's karaoke machine! The Martians were furious! Dad's told Mum

It's The Great Escape all over again!

he's going to get a new pet. Mum said that was OK so long as it wasn't another

STOP THAT RACKET!

♯ ♩ ♪ Happy days are here again...! ♪ ♩ ♭

alligator or a snake or anything with too many teeth. Dad's getting it tomorrow. I've no idea what it will be.

19 What's That?

The new pet is here. It's a bird and it looks
a bit scraggy to me. Even Mum thinks so.
She asked Dad why did it have such a big
head and neck?

    'Vultures always look like that,'
said Dad.

    Mum's voice went all high and
squeaky. 'VULTURE?' she squawked.
'THAT'S A VULTURE?'

    Mum's not speaking to Dad any more.
Oh well, here we go again...

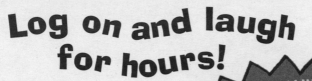

14½ Things You Didn't Know About

Jeremy Strong

* * * * * * * * * * * * * * * * *

1. He loves eating liquorice.

2. He used to like diving. He once dived from the high board and his trunks came off!

3. He used to play electric violin in a rock band called **THE INEDIBLE CHEESE SANDWICH**.

4. He got a 100-metre swimming certificate when he couldn't even swim.

5. When he was five, he sat on a heater and burnt his bottom.

6. Jeremy used to look after a dog that kept eating his underpants. (No – NOT while he was wearing them!)

7. When he was five, he left a basin tap running with the plug in and flooded the bathroom.

8. He can make his ears waggle.

9. He has visited over a thousand schools.

10. He once scored minus ten in an exam! That's ten less than nothing!

11. His hair has gone grey, but his mind hasn't.

12. He'd like to have a pet tiger.

13. He'd like to learn the piano.

14. He has dreadful handwriting.

And a half . . . His favourite hobby is sleeping. He's very good at it.

Woofy hi! I'm Streaker, the fastest dog in the world. My owner, Trevor, thinks he can train me to obey him. The trouble is even I don't know what I'm going to do next! I don't know what SIT or STOP mean, and I do get into some big scrapes. We almost got arrested once! This is the first book about me and it's almost as funny and fast as I am!

LAUGH YOUR SOCKS OFF WITH

THE HUNDRED-MILE-AN-HOUR DOG

Available Now!

* * * * * * * * * * * * * * * * * * *

I'm Jamie. I am going to be the world's greatest film director when I grow up. I'm trying to make a film about a cartoon cow I've invented called KRAZY KOW. However, making a film isn't as easy as you might think. How was I to know everyone would see the bit where I caught my big sister snogging Justin? How was I to know the exploding strawberries would make quite so much mess? How was I to know my big bro's football kit would turn pink? And why did everyone have to blame ME?

LAUGH YOUR SOCKS OFF WITH

KRAZY KOW SAVES THE WORLD – WELL, ALMOST

Available Now!